MALLORY COX AND THE VIKING BOX

Everything around Mallory went hazy, swirly and cold. "Where are my magic socks taking me now?" he wondered.

It wasn't long before he found out. He landed – FLUMP! – on board a long, wooden ship. There was a mast with a furled sail and a load of men, seated on wooden benches and rowing lustily. They wore leather jerkins and breeches of coarse cloth.

"Hmm!" Mallory said to himself. "If you ask me, I've been taken back to Viking times, and things have taken a bit of a ticklish turn! If only I could speak Viking, I could explain that I'm a harmless tourist who just wants a good nose around!"

One of the men stood up and approached Mallory. His shoulders were broader than a Wendy House.

"Dash and diddle!" cried Mallory. He pointed at himself and bawled, "MALLORY! ME, FRIEND! NICE MALLORY! YOU NO HURT!"

The man stared at Mallory for what seemed a long time and then said: "You've got a really weird hairdo. And where did you get those clothes from? They're terrible!"

**Also by the same author,
and available in Knight Books:**

Mallory Cox and his Magic Socks

Mallory Cox and the Viking Box

by Andrew Matthews

illustrated by Tony Ross

KNIGHT BOOKS
Hodder and Stoughton

First published in Great Britain in 1991 by J. M. Dent & Sons Ltd.
Knight edition published 1992

The characters and situations in this book are entirely imaginary and bear no relation to any real person or actual happenings.

British Library C.I.P.

A catalogue record for this book is available from the British Library

ISBN 0 340 56813 5

Printed and bound in Great Britain for Hodder and Stoughton Children's Books, a division of Hodder and Stoughton Ltd., Mill Road, Dunton Green Sevenoaks, Kent TN13 2YA. (Editorial Office: 47 Bedford Square, London WC1B 3DP) by Cox & Wyman Ltd., Reading.

For Shani and Sasha

-1-

Bored at Breakfast

Most people have secrets, but Mallory Cox had a really amazing secret! His Great Aunt Enid from up North, who was more than a bit on the witchy side, had given Mallory a pair of magic socks as a ninth birthday present. When Mallory put them on, anything could happen.

When he wasn't wearing his magic socks, Mallory was just like any other nine-year-old boy, so it was very frustrating that his parents wouldn't let him tell any of his friends about his magic socks. They wouldn't even let him wear them to school. Mallory was only allowed to put them on at weekends and he had to stay in the house or garden.

"After all, if you went out and something magic happened," Mr Cox warned, "it might also happen to people standing near you. Not everybody likes to have magic doings, Mallory."

This rule was all very well at first, but after a bit it got on Mallory's nerves. The problem was that his two favourite hobbies were fiddling about and nosing around. Fiddling about was quite easy at home, but nosing around was a different matter. Mallory had nosed around the house and garden until there was nothing interesting left.

One cold, damp Saturday morning, Mallory stumped downstairs into the kitchen. Mr Cox was toasting bread and Mrs Cox was folding

sheets of newspaper into the shapes of farm-yard animals. She was half-way through a goat when Mallory came in. He barged through the door so loudly that Mrs Cox jumped and ripped off one of the goat's legs.

"Good morning, Mallory," she sighed.

"Humph!" Mallory replied.

"Good morning, Mallory," said Mr Cox, catching two slices of toast as they came twanging out of the toaster.

"Pumph!" said Mallory as he slumped into a chair and pulled a sulky face.

Mr Cox looked at Mallory and raised one eyebrow. "Is anything wrong?" he asked.

"I'm fed up!" Mallory announced. "It's too cold and misty to fiddle about in the garden shed and I've run out of things to nose around. The only thing left to do is be in a bad mood so that's what I'm doing. In fact, I'm in such a bad mood that I may throw a tantrum at any moment!"

"I do hope not, dear," said Mrs Cox as she set about folding the three-legged goat into a turkey. "Your tantrums are such loud affairs!"

"Of course," Mallory said slyly, "if I went out for a walk with my magic socks on, I'd be sure of having a really interesting time."

"How many times must I tell you, Mallory," Mr Cox reproved as he spread a slice of buttered toast with quince preserve, "magic isn't everybody's cup of tea. Apart from anything else, it's dangerous!"

"Bumph!" snorted Mallory. "I don't see what's so dangerous about it."

This was quite a big fib. At various times while wearing his magic socks, Mallory had been chased by a dinosaur, mixed up in a battle of magic between two witches, captured by pirates, bound by brigands and almost swallowed by a whale. He hadn't mentioned these adventures to his parents – or they would most

certainly have taken the socks away from him.

"I can see we're going to have to do some-thing to take your mind off those socks of yours," said Mr Cox. "I suggest a family out-ing to the Museum of Local History."

"Grumph!" grumbled Mallory. "If you ask me, that doesn't sound very interesting!"

"You could always tidy your bedroom instead, dear," suggested Mrs Cox, pressing the turkey's wattles flat with her thumb.

"Oh, drat!" scowled Mallory. "Maybe going to the museum isn't such a bad idea after all."

-2-

Mooching in the Museum

The Museum of Local History wasn't a terribly exciting-looking place. It was in the Town Hall, next door to the public library. In the entrance hall there were three glass tanks. One contained a stickleback. The second was occupied by a disgruntled-looking toad squatting beside a saucer of worms. According to a label, the third tank was supposed to have a great crested newt in it. All Mallory could see was water, pondweed and a rock. Next to the invisible newt was a glass case with a stone in it. *This stone*, a notice informed Mallory, *was tripped over by Charles Dickens when he got off at the local station in error on 2 December 1867.*

"Boring," groaned Mallory. "Boring, boring, boring!"

"Hello!" said Mr Cox. "What's this?"

He nodded to a sign that read: *Discoveries from the recent Ajax cinema car-park dig.*

"Oh, that!" yawned Mallory. "There was a lot of blah about that in school. They didn't find treasure or skeletons or anything interesting."

"But it's local history, dear," insisted Mrs Cox as she folded a museum guide pamphlet into a dachshund. "Local history is always interesting."

"Hah!" said Mallory.

The Cox family followed the arrow on the sign into a room that was filled with tatty-looking stuffed animals.

"If you ask me," murmured Mallory, "these animals aren't stuffed at all, they're bored stiff! I'll end up like them if I stay in here much longer!"

At that moment Mallory saw a sign to the museum toilets and his face lit up with a wicked smile.

"Oh, dear!" he exclaimed. "I want to go to the loo all of a sudden!"

"But you went before we left the house!" protested Mr Cox.

"Yes, and now I want to go again."

"Very well," frowned Mr Cox, "but don't take all day."

"Next time you go before we leave the house, remember to go twice, dear," advised

Mrs Cox, turning the dachshund into Lord Nelson. "Then, if you need to go again while you're out, you'll find you've already been."

Mallory skipped to the loo. As soon as he was inside he rubbed his hands together gleefully.

"I've got just the thing to liven this old museum up a bit!" he chuckled. He reached into his anorak pocket and brought out the magic socks.

No one would have guessed the socks were magic from looking at them. They appeared to be a pair of ordinary, plain, grey socks. But Mallory knew that they were far from ordinary. They had been knitted from dragon's wool and when the magic in them started working, they turned all sorts of wild and wacky colours with incredible patterns that kept on changing: signs of the zodiac, ringed planets, winged horses and all sorts. For some unknown reason, the magic shock waves did some pretty peculiar things to the colour of Mallory's hair as well. Despite this, Mallory changed into his magic socks faster than a hedgehog rolling downstairs and rushed off to find his parents. He found them peering into a tall case lined with glass shelves. Next to it was a notice-board festooned with photo-

graphs of holes in the ground and a notice reading: *Exciting new discoveries reveal ancient Viking settlement.*

"Bunkum and fiddlesticks!" scoffed Mallory. "Most boring exhibition in the world would be more like it!" He glanced at his socks, but they were still grey. "Nothing doing yet," he told himself. "I may as well mooch for a bit."

The first exhibit in the case was a rusty pin about five centimetres long. *Viking pin* said a label.

"Bah!" said Mallory.

A mangled slice of Christmas pudding next to the pin turned out to be the remains of a Viking sandal.

"Pah!" said Mallory. "This isn't what I call exciting! If you ask me, a packet of dolly mixtures is more exciting than this!"

But the next exhibit stopped his grumbling. It was a square of beautifully carved bone.

Viking box lid, said the label, *carved from narwhal ivory*.

"A-a-h!" said Mallory.

The bone carvings showed warriors and wolves and dragons with twisty tails that looped and whirled and turned into hair and leaves.

"Pity they didn't find the rest of it! I wonder what a Viking would have kept in a box like that?" pondered Mallory.

"Mallory!" said Mr Cox in a severe tone. "You're wearing your magic socks!"

"How did you know?" gasped Mallory.

"Because your hair has gone a revolting shade of red!" snapped Mr Cox.

Mallory looked down at his socks. They were glowing bright blue and sparkling spirals and cubes were twirling around in them. They

started to quiver and tingle against his skin in a way that made Mallory check to see if chilled millepedes were marching around his ankles.

"Take those socks off this instant!" barked Mr Cox.

But before Mallory could do as he was told, colour started to drain out of everything. The museum began to fade and before long, Mallory found that he was standing somewhere completely different.

- 3 -

Larks on the Long Ship

Everything around Mallory went hazy, swirly and cold.

"Where are my magic socks taking me now?" he wondered.

It wasn't long before he found out. He landed – FLUMP! – on board a long, wooden ship. The ship had a tall, curved prow. There was a mast with a furled sail and a load of men, seated on wooden benches and rowing lustily. They wore leather jerkins and breeches of coarse cloth.

All the men were bearded and shouting, "Hup, ya! Hup, ya!" to keep time with the oars.

Unfortunately, Mallory's arrival was so startling that some men went: "Hup!" while others were going: "Ya!" The oars knocked into one another, people fell over and the ship started going round in a circle.

The men stared at Mallory in silence.

"Hmm!" Mallory said to himself. "If you ask me, I've been taken back to Viking times, and things have taken a bit of a ticklish turn! If only I could speak Viking, I could explain that I'm a harmless tourist who just wants a good nose around!"

One of the men stood up and approached Mallory. He had long, fair hair woven into plaits, and piercing blue eyes. There was a gold band round one of his forearms, and a sword at his belt. His shoulders were broader than a Wendy House.

"Dash and diddle!" cried Mallory. He pointed at himself and bawled, "MALLORY! ME, FRIEND! NICE MALLORY! YOU NO HURT!"

The man stared at Mallory for what seemed a long time and then said: "You've got a really weird hairdo. And where did you get those clothes from? They're terrible!"

Mallory was so amazed that one flick of a tadpole's tail would have knocked him flying.

"You can talk!" he yelped.

"What did you expect me to do?" the man asked. "Grunt like an elk?"

"I mean, you can talk English!"

"What's English?" frowned the man.

"It's the language we're speaking!"

"But we're talking Viking," said the man, giving Mallory a funny look.

Mallory thought hard, "This must have something to do with the magic in my socks," he decided. "Er, what's your name, then?" he asked the man. He tried to sound as friendly as he could be under the circumstances.

The man thumped himself on the chest and proudly proclaimed, "I am Harald Hardaxe, son of Leif Wolfthrottler and Inga the Singer!"

"Gosh!" gulped Mallory. He was impressed, but determined not to be outdone. He thumped himself on the chest, coughed and said, "I am Mallory, son of Clive and Patricia Cox!"

Harald Hardaxe put his hand to his sword in a threatening way.

"What are you doing on my ship?" he demanded.

"Hitching a ride," said Mallory. "It's quicker than swimming and much drier too."

"But where did you come from?" asked Harald.

"Oh, you know," shrugged Mallory, "around."

The oarsmen were pointing at Mallory and muttering among themselves.

"He's an elf!" shouted one.

"He's a spirit sent by Odin!" called another.

"Tish and tosh!" scoffed Mallory. "I'm a boy! I'm a bit tall for my age, but that's not my fault! There's no reason to go making a huge fuss over a little thing like my appearing suddenly out of thin air! I'm just a boy and you're great big strapping chaps! Huh! I thought Vikings were supposed to be fierce warriors who were frightened of nothing!"

"I'm not too keen on cockroaches!" confessed the helmsman.

"Cockroaches aren't so bad," an oarsman told him. "But spiders! Ugh!"

"All right, men!" Harald snapped. "The boy does have a point. There's no need to be afraid of a skinny little shrimp like him! Let's pick up our oars and get home to Narborg!"

-4-

Nordic Niff

The long ship glided through the dark
waters of a narrow fiord. The creaking
of the oars and the loud, "Hup, ya! Hup, ya!"
of the rowing men echoed off rocky cliffs.
Mallory stood beside Harald Hardaxe just
behind the dragon's head prow and tried to
look as though a Viking voyage was something that happened to him every day.

The ship rounded a headland. In the distance
Mallory saw a beach that was the colour of
the inside of a Hoover bag and a group of
thatched huts huddled closer together than a
family of sleeping gerbils.

"I wonder what poor wretches used to live
in those derelict hovels?" Mallory mused.

"Look, men!" Harald called. "Home is in
sight!"

There was loud cheering.

"Home?" puzzled Mallory. "What home?"

Harald pointed to the huts. "That's Narborg, our home town! It's the biggest town for miles around. People save up all year to take their holidays there!"

"Fancy that!" said Mallory, although he didn't fancy it at all. The wind blew a smell into Mallory's face that made his eyes water.

Harald Hardaxe took a deep breath and sighed blissfully.

"Ah, the smell of home!" he said. "There's nothing else like it! It's said that voyagers can

smell Narborg leagues and leagues before it comes into sight."

"That doesn't surprise me!" commented Mallory.

From a distance Narborg looked and smelled awful. Close-up it was worse. The long ship drew up at a quayside that was piled high with old nets and bits of rotting fish. A few people were waiting on the quay and when Harald Hardaxe jumped ashore, one of them came running up and hugged him.

It was a girl with wildly flowing fair hair and plump cheeks, scattered with freckles. She wore a grey woollen shift and there was a serious-looking knife tucked into the rope belt around her waist. Mallory guessed that she was about the same age as he was.

"Father," the girl asked Harald inquisitively, "who is the strange boy with green hair?"

"His name is Mallory," Harald said. "He is our guest and we must greet him with traditional Viking hospitality. We must have a feast with plenty of roast oxen and lots of beer!"

"Ya!" cheered the long ship crew.

"But Father!" cried the girl. "I've come with an urgent message! You and the men have to go to the mountains at once. The Snorrisen brothers are feuding again ... and they're coming this way!"

"By the lips of Loki, they're early this year!" gasped Harald.

"Mallory, my daughter will take you to visit my home. Men, we'll have to leave our plunder in the boat and pick it up later! If we're not quick, the Snorrisens might do each other a terrible injury!"

With terrific speed the crew organized themselves into ranks of three behind Harald Hardaxe and went running off down the quayside.

Mallory and Harald's daughter looked curiously at one another.

"Mallory," said the girl. "That's a funny name."

"Oh?" Mallory replied. "What's your name, then?"

"I am Gerda Ravenhair, daughter of Harald Hardaxe and Freya the Slayer!" the girl announced.

"Ravenhair?" sniggered Mallory. "Why are you called Ravenhair when your hair is fair?"

"Mother is terribly short-sighted! All the other children make fun of me because of my name." Gerda said miserably. "Come on, I'll show you the way to my home."

The main street of Narborg was thick with mud. Small children and yapping dogs chased around the steaming rubbish piled outside every hut.

"I'b nebber seen anythigg like this in by life before!" croaked Mallory, holding his nose.

"Ah!" grinned Gerda. "Not everybody is lucky enough to live in an up-to-date place like Narborg!"

She stopped in front of a particularly ramshackle hut with a sagging roof.

"Mother!" she called sweetly. "Are you within?"

"Gerda?" screeched a voice which was squeakier than toe-nails scraping on a zinc bath. "Where are you?"

A filthy woman in equally filthy clothes appeared in the doorway of the hut, fanning herself with a dried fish. She squinted at Mallory through a knotted mass of red hair.

"There you are, my daughter!" she cried and before he could protest, the woman gathered Mallory up in her arms and gave him a kiss on the cheek that turned his hair the colour of custard powder.

-5-

Outraged Olaf

When Freya the Slayer discovered her mistake, she laughed loudly and spread her hands out in a gesture of greeting.

"Come inside and accept our hospitality!" she proclaimed. "It's an old Viking custom to greet people with food."

Mallory wasn't keen on this idea, but with Freya pulling and Gerda pushing him, he didn't have any choice.

A peat fire smouldered in the centre of the hut's earth floor. Hanging over the fire was a small iron cauldron. There was something disgusting bubbling menacingly inside it. Brown, withered fish hung from strings tied to the rafters.

"Would you like a smoked herring?" Freya asked Mallory.

"Ah . . ." he said. "Well, the thing is . . ."

"A soused herring?" continued Freya. "A pickled herring? I could fry a fresh herring for you, unless you'd prefer a boiled one. Or perhaps you'd rather have some soup?"

"What kind of soup?" asked Mallory.

"Salted herring soup! It's delicious, even though I say it myself!" beamed Freya.

"There's no need to go to any trouble ..." Mallory mumbled.

"It's no trouble!" Freya assured him. "I've already cooked some up for my husband Harald. He's gone to the mountains to see to the Snorrisen brothers. Feuding always gives a man a good appetite!"

Mallory had to give in. He sat on an old pine stump near the door and watched helplessly as Freya stirred the contents of the cauldron. It was so thick she had to use both hands on the spoon. Gerda sat down on the ground near him and smiled.

"When I grow up, I'll live in a hut just like this and I'll be able to do all the things I like best, without people telling me off for it!"

"And what do you like doing best?" asked Mallory, trying to keep his mind off the soup.

"Fiddling about!" replied Gerda. "And when I'm not fiddling about, I like to nose around."

"Why, so do I!" cried Mallory. He was genuinely interested now. "You'd love the town I live in! Nosing around is much more fun there – it's less smelly and there's billions of things to fiddle about with! There's milk-bottle tops and hair-grips, the insides of old radios, ball-bearings, springs, bicycle pumps, rubber-bands, ring-pulls off cans, pheasant feathers, batteries, magnets ..." This was the start of a long list that completely bewildered Gerda, as she didn't have the faintest idea what Mallory was talking about. She smiled and nodded anyway, so as not to hurt his feelings.

"Other kids don't seem to be interested in that sort of thing, though," Mallory confessed with a sigh. "They call me a show-off and a know-it-all!"

"It's the same here!" Gerda told him. "All people ever say to me is 'mind your own business'. You're the only other person I've met who enjoys nosing and fiddling!"

"Fancy!" gasped Mallory. "That must mean we're friends! Shall we shake hands?"

"What do you mean?" puzzled Gerda.

"Where I come from," Mallory explained, "when two people make friends, they hold hands and shake them up and down."

"When Vikings make friends," said Gerda, "they cut their thumbs with daggers and let their blood mix together in a bowl."

"Maybe we're not friends *quite* yet!" Mallory said quickly.

"Here we are!" shouted Freya, ladling a grey splodge from the cauldron into a wooden bowl. "Come, Gerda! Stop this talking and serve our guest his food!"

Gerda scrambled to her feet, took the bowl from Freya, stuck a bone spoon into it and handed it to Mallory with a wink.

"Mother's slipped you a couple of fish-heads as a special treat!" she gurgled. "I think she's taken a liking to you!"

Mallory looked into the bowl, cringed and wondered how Freya treated people she *didn't* like. He knew he'd never be able to eat any of the soup, but he didn't want to offend his new-found friend or her mother. He waited until Freya and Gerda were busy serving up their own portions and sneakily threw the contents of his bowl out into the street. He heard it splatter as it landed, and then, to his surprise and alarm, he heard a loud bellowing and spluttering.

"Has someone offended a water buffalo?" Mallory asked himself. But then, all of a sudden, he realized the sounds were being made by a person, because a deep voice shouted:

"By Odin's nostrils! Who dares to offer an insult to Olaf Ironhammer?"

"I wonder what's got into Olaf?" said Freya. "He's in a terrible mood. It's his turn to keep guard in the town while all the other men are feuding with the Snorrisens, and he hates missing all the fun!"

There was a sound of heavy footsteps squelching closer through the mud and then a huge shape loomed in the doorway.

-6-

Block-busting Boasts

Gerda and Freya screamed and Mallory whirled around. The man in the doorway was over six feet tall and had a ginger beard that bristled like a fighting cat. He wore a woollen jerkin, leather leggings, a wolfskin cloak, a horned helmet ... and a bowlful of salted herring soup. There was a fish-head stuck to the tip of one of the horns on his helmet. He shook a fist the size of a loaf into the hut.

"Who did this to me?" he roared.

"I did!" said Mallory, thinking fast. "I thought it was an old Viking custom to greet people with food."

Olaf Ironhammer stared at Mallory and went pale with horror.

"By the thighs of Thor, it's a bog-troll!" he gasped.

Mallory didn't know what a bog-troll was, but being called names made him angry. He jumped to his feet: "I'm not!"

"Then why are you wearing those terrible robes?" shouted Olaf. "And why does your hair keep changing colour? And why have you got windows in front of your eyes?"

"You can talk!" Mallory replied. "Why have you got a helmet with horns on? In my *Bumper Book Of Facts That Make Other People Look Stupid* it says that real Vikings *never* wore horned helmets!"

"Oh, Ragnarok!" hissed Olaf, tearing off his helmet and hurling it over his shoulder.

"That lying helmet-trader told me horns were all the rage! But it doesn't alter the fact that you've offended the great Olaf Ironhammer, the man who can throw a plough-ox from one side of the fiord to the other!"

Mallory, still fuming, was determined not to be out-boasted.

"That's nothing!" he sneered. "I can walk all the way from my house to the supermarket without stepping on a single crack in the pavement!"

Olaf narrowed his eyes: "I can wrestle two brown bears at once and beat them both!"

"Piff and poff!" mocked Mallory. "I can read four library books in a week!"

Olaf reached into his cloak and pulled out something Mallory found oddly familiar. It was a lidless bone box, carved with dragons and wolves and warriors. "This is the box I keep my powdered-herring snuff in!" announced Olaf. "I carved it from a narwhal's tusk and I caught the narwhal single-handed! But I lost the lid on a little pillaging holiday overseas," he added sadly.

Mallory pointed at the breast pocket of his anorak. "This is the Blue Peter badge I got for collecting silver paper!" he informed Olaf.

"So!" Olaf snarled through clenched teeth. "You seem to have a high opinion of yourself!"

"I'm the only one in my class who knows the thirteen-times-table," boasted Mallory, getting carried away.

"And how good are you when it comes to single combat?" growled Olaf. "Fighting face-to-face with double-headed battleaxes while balancing on a plank set over a pit of fiery lava?"

"U-u-u-u-m," went Mallory.

Gerda saw that she was in danger of losing her only friend almost as soon as she had met him. She bustled forward and put a protective hand on Mallory's shoulder.

"Go away, Olaf Ironhammer!" she shrilled. "Stop bullying our guest and leave us in peace!"

"Hold your tongue, little sprat!" thundered Olaf. He reached out his huge, hairy hand towards Mallory, but Mallory ducked and dodged. Olaf turned and Gerda kicked him on the shin.

"Why you . . . !" roared Olaf.

Mallory ran out into the street. Olaf ran out after him, followed by Gerda. She overtook the enraged warrior and stood shoulder-to-shoulder with Mallory.

"We'll face the blundering old walrus together!" she snarled.

"Don't play too roughly, Gerda dear!" Freya called from the doorstep. "You know how easy it is to hurt a man's pride!"

Mallory gulped as Olaf produced a double-headed axe and trundled towards him. For a moment, he wished that his witchy Aunt Enid from up North was there to help with some magic. Then he remembered that the last time he'd seen her, she'd been a green jelly rabbit in the middle of a war of spells with Gussie, his other witchy aunt. Mallory decided that a green jelly rabbit wasn't really much use against a large, hairy Viking with a sharp axe.

With a fearsome cry, Olaf swung the weapon round and round his head. "Prepare to be smorgasbord!" he thundered.

And at that moment, much to Mallory's relief, his socks started tingling and Olaf Ironhammer's ugly, soup-stained face began to fade. The huts of Narborg became transparent and through them Mallory could see the fami-

liar outline of the museum growing clearer every second.

"Phew!" he breathed. "That big bully was jolly lucky my socks brought me back when they did. If I'd really lost my temper, I would have shown him what's what ... er, oh dear!"

Mallory had just realized that his parents were still waiting for him. Mr Cox had his arms folded across his chest and was tapping his right foot in an impatient way.

"About time!" he rasped. "Really, Mallory, if you think your mother and I have got nothing better to do than to – " He broke

off, his eyes rounder than goldfish bowls. "Who's that?" he demanded.

"Eh?" squeaked Mallory. He turned his head and saw Gerda standing behind him, her hand still clutching his shoulder.

"Where am I?" she cried.

"How did that happen?" exclaimed Mallory.

"Who is this strange girl?" demanded Mr Cox.

"What have you been up to, Mallory dear?" enquired Mrs Cox. She leaned closer to Mallory and whispered, "I must say, your young friend does have strange taste in clothes!"

Gerda was staring in pale bewilderment at the glass case in front of her.

"Mallory!" she hissed. "Look! There – next to that old sandal!"

A museum attendant appeared, drawn by the sound of raised voices.

"You can't argue in here, I'm afraid, sir!" he told Mr Cox. "This is a museum. If you wish to continue your altercation you'll have to go elsewhere. Try the library next door."

Red with embarrassment, Mr Cox led his family and Gerda outside.

Traffic Terror

Outside the museum Mr Cox acted like a champion sheep-dog. He herded everybody into the peaceful square around the corner where there was a statue of Queen Victoria.

"Mallory, what was the lid of Olaf's herring-snuff box doing there?" Gerda asked.

"I thought I recognized that box of his when he showed it to me!" said Mallory. "Hey, Dad! I know just what Vikings used their bone boxes for!"

"Stop showing-off, Mallory. This is not the time to discuss your theories on Viking bone boxes. I'm much more interested in who this girl is!" Mr Cox said tersely.

"Her name is Gerda. She's from Viking times!" Mallory said.

If Mr Cox had been a saucepan, he would have boiled.

"Viking times?" he steamed. "But she doesn't belong here! You must take her back at once!"

"I can't, I don't know how to!" complained Mallory. "Anyway, I don't want her to go back yet. She's my friend. I've never had a friend before!"

Mr Cox was so annoyed that he tapped both feet at once and nearly fell over. "We can't discuss the matter here, but before we go any further, you're to take off those aggravating socks!"

"I won't be able to understand Gerda if I do that," protested Mallory.

While this discussion was going on, Gerda had a good look round at her surroundings and she became pale and quiet. There were tall buildings that reminded her of the cliffs of the fiord – except that the cliffs didn't have windows in them. The statue in the square alarmed her the most.

"What happened to that lady?" she asked Mallory.

"She used to be queen," Mallory replied.

"Why did they turn her into stone?"

"Right!" Mr Cox declared loudly. "We must get Gerda back to the house and into a bath as soon as possible."

"A bath?" exclaimed Mallory.

"Your friend does smell a bit of fish, dear," said Mrs Cox discreetly.

"A bit?" hooted Mr Cox. "She whiffs like the inside of a trawler! To the car-park, everyone! And if anybody stares or passes remarks, smile and try to act normally."

Mr Cox turned on his heel, took two paces forward and collided with a policeman, who was on his way to the nearby police station.

"Steady on, sir!" said the policeman.

"Er, good monstering conable – I mean, good morning constable!" gabbled Mr Cox.

"Everything all right, sir?" asked the policeman, staring in amazement at Mallory's hair and Gerda's clothes.

"Perfectly!" said Mr Cox. "We've just finished the family shopping and we're off home!"

The policeman shook his head and tutted as he watched the Coxes and Gerda walk off.

"The kids of today!" he said to himself. "What do they think they look like!"

As soon as they left the square, Gerda started to tremble. The streets were crowded with Saturday shoppers. The traffic terrified her. Exhaust fumes made her cough, and whenever a car beeped its horn or a big lorry rattled by, she jumped with alarm. The noise of an express train roaring past made her clap her hands over her ears. Everything was terrifying – and when Concorde flew overhead tearing the sky in half

with its roaring engines, Gerda panicked. She
gave a loud cry and bolted into a run which
would have done credit to the favourite on
Grand National Day.

"Quick, Mallory!" urged Mr Cox. "Catch
her before she runs into the road and has an
accident!"

Gerda had no clear idea in her mind where
she was running to. She only knew that the
place Mallory had brought her to was strange
and loud and frightening. She missed Narborg
and desperately wanted to clutch at anything
that would remind her of it. With streaming
hair and wild eyes, she galloped back into the
museum and rushed down corridors until she
came to the room containing the Viking ex-

hibits. Mallory, close behind, saw her open up the glass case and reach inside.

"Hey!" he cried. "You musn't do that! Those things belong to the museum!"

"This belongs to Olaf!" Gerda shouted crossly, holding up the carved box lid. "It shouldn't be here in this terrible place!" Mallory caught up with Gerda and leaned against her, panting.

"You don't understand – " he began, but he never finished what he was going to say. As he was speaking, he felt the milk-and-rice-crispies-in-his-shoes feeling of the magic socks going to work. For the second time that day, he saw the museum walls start to fade. There was no doubt about it, the magic socks were off again!

-8-

Olaf Overjoyed

Mallory and Gerda were surrounded by a swirling grey mist, through which the outskirts of Narborg appeared. The huts became more and more clear as the mist gradually vanished.

"Home!" yelled Gerda. "Oh, I'm so relieved to be – " She broke off with a cry of alarm.

All was not well in Narborg. In the main street, a small war seemed to have started. A great crowd of people were bashing each other with whatever came to hand, while all around dogs barked in distress and little children cried in fear.

In the centre of the crowd stood two gigantic, fair-haired men, fighting one another with swords and shields and making a terrific clatter. Mallory recognized Harald Hardaxe and his crew. Olaf Ironhammer was there too – his helmet was dented and one of his eyes had been blackened. Freya the Slayer stood at the edge of the crowd, throwing handfuls of lukewarm salted herring soup over everyone.

"It's the Snorrisen brothers! They must have reached Narborg before anyone could stop them!" wailed Gerda. "Oh, make them stop, Mallory!"

"Me?" croaked Mallory, feeling rather worried.

"You made the magic to take us away from Narborg and bring us back! Can't you make magic now?" pleaded Gerda.

"Well ... um ... I could give it a go, I suppose," said Mallory. 'After all,' he thought to
himself, 'the magic socks have made sure I
haven't come to any real harm ... so far!'

He cleared his throat and said in a very loud
voice, "Just stop it! Behave yourselves this
minute!"

The crowd turned, looked and fell silent in
astonishment at the sight of the strangely-
dressed boy with the multi-coloured hair.
"You should be ashamed of yourselves!" Mallory told them. "You're all grown-ups! You're
supposed to set an example to your children,
not frighten them out of their jim-jams!"

With a couple of snarls, the two fair-haired men elbowed their way to the front of the crowd and glared at Mallory.

"Who dares to interrupt me in mid-feud, brother Siguf?" demanded the one on the left.

"It was this troublesome sea-squirt, brother Solmund!" replied the one on the right. "By the breath of Balder, I was just starting to enjoy myself when he came along and spoiled everything. Shall we vent all our Nordic fury on him, brother Solmund?"

"Of course!" cried Solmund. "If we don't tear this troublesome stranger to shreds, folk will start saying that the Snorrisen brothers have turned all goody-goody!"

Bellowing fiercely, the Snorrisens approached Mallory, swooshing their swords around their heads.

Mallory searched frantically in his pockets for anything that might help and found two marbles and an elastic band.

"I warn you!" he said. "I may have to play tough if you come any closer!"

"Y-a-a-a-h!" yelled the brothers as they broke into a run.

Mallory crouched down and expertly flicked the marbles onto the ground with his thumb. Solmund trod on the marbles, slipped

and fell face-down with a thump that made the earth shake. Siguf tripped over his brother and landed with a bone-crunching crash.

Mallory quickly hooked one end of the elastic band over his left thumb and pulled it tight with his right hand.

"Have you had enough, or do I have to flick you with this?" he asked grimly.

Solmund was too dazed and winded to reply. Siguf waved his bent sword wearily.

"You win!" he mumbled. "By Odin, I'm glad you're no son of mine! You're going to be a real handful when you get older!" He raised himself onto one elbow, wincing with pain, and shouted: "That's it! The feuding sea-

son's over! Back to fishing for herring tomorrow!"

Some of the crowd cheered when they heard this news, some groaned and scowled in a disappointed way. Olaf Ironhammer ran over to Mallory and gave him a slap on the back that made his ears ring.

"Thor's thunderbolts, you've shown some spirit, boy!" he proclaimed. "I'm willing to forget all about that faceful of herring soup you gave me!"

"And that's not all Mallory is going to give you," said Gerda, holding up the carved bone lid. "He went to a lot of trouble to get this back for you."

"Wonderful! My box lid!" bawled Olaf. "Now I won't keep spilling snuff everywhere and making people sneeze!" He jogged off to show the lid to Freya and Harald.

Gerda turned to Mallory with a happy smile.

"I'm really glad to be home," she said. "I couldn't stand living in your town! It's far too crowded and noisy, and men look funny without beards!"

"And I couldn't stand to live in Narborg," admitted Mallory. "The food is diabolical and – oh-ho!"

He felt his ankles tickling and tingling as the magic socks glowed.

"Here I go again! Goodbye, Gerda!" he said. "Goodbye, Olaf!"

The mist gathered so quickly that he didn't get a chance to hear their replies. The magic socks took Mallory from Narborg straight back to the museum ... where he found his parents were waiting for him.

Mr Cox would not accept any excuses – he made Mallory take off his magic socks and put his ordinary ones back on there and then.

"You see what comes of meddling with magic, Mallory?" Mr Cox said as they left the museum and walked towards the car-park. "That poor girl might have been hurt!"

"Oh, poohs!" sulked Mallory. "It was nice to have a Viking friend, even if it was only for a little while. And she got home safely in the end!"

"What you need is to take up a nice, quiet hobby dear," said Mrs Cox, searching in her bag for a sheet of newspaper. "Like building model aeroplanes, or stamp collecting, or playing the tuba!"

"Perhaps you're right!" sighed Mallory. "Wearing a pair of magic socks is a bit alarming at times!"

"I'm delighted to hear you say so!" said Mr Cox. "If you carry on, who knows what you might turn up with next? I mean, a young Viking girl was all very well, but suppose you returned from one of your magic jaunts with a creature from another world? Whatever would your mother and I say to the neighbours?"

Mallory went all quiet and goggly-eyed.

"A creature from another world, eh?" he mumbled. "I wonder what kind of friend that would make?"

"Oh, blow!" moaned Mr Cox. "When will I learn to keep my big mouth shut?"

David Tinkler

THE SCOURGE OF THE DINNER LADIES

Chomp chomp burp slurp . . .

This was the noise of dinner time. Nobody
dared to talk.
'Who was that?' yelled Mrs Sludge.
'WHO WAS WHISPERING?'

There were some tough new dinner ladies at
Littlesprat Primary School: the Granny
Fang Gang. Mrs Sludge was the roughest,
toughest dinner lady that there had ever
been. And now she was brandishing her
ladle!

Could the pupils of Littlesprat survive the
Scourge of the Dinner Ladies?

These are the adventures of the famous
Black Stallion and his friend Alec that are
available in Knight

Walter Farley
The Black Stallion
The Black Stallion Revolts
The Black Stallion Returns
The Black Stallion and Satan
Son of the Black Stallion
Black Stallion's Courage
The Black Stallion's Filly
The Black Stallion Mystery
The Black Stallion and Flame
The Black Stallion's Ghost
The Black Stallion's Challenge
The Black Stallion and the Stranger
The Black Stallion Legend
The Young Black Stallion

Rolf Harris

YOUR CARTOON TIME

Did you know that you can draw?

Rolf Harris shows you how – clearly and simply – in YOUR CARTOON TIME. Starting with stick figures, he explains how to develop these step-by-step into your own stylish characters, and there are ideas too for how you can use your drawings – as birthday cards, home movies and so on.

Drawing is fun!

All you need is a pencil, paper and Rolf Harris's book – YOUR CARTOON TIME.

MORE GREAT BOOKS AVAILABLE FROM KNIGHT

39223 1	YOUR CARTOON TIME Rolf Harris	£2.99
54875 4	FIVE ON A TREASURE ISLAND	
	Enid Blyton	£2.99
19687 4	THE BLACK STALLION Walter Farley	£2.99
40860 X	THE WRESTLING PRINCESS	
	Judy Corbalis	£2.99
04136 6	JILL'S GYMKHANA Ruby Ferguson	£2.99
54722 7	MALLORY COX AND HIS MAGIC SOCKS	
	Andrew Matthews	£2.99
16303 8	AMAZON ADVENTURE Willard Price	£2.99
50166 9	THE SCOURGE OF THE DINNER LADIES	
	David Tinkler	£2.50

All these books are available at your local bookshop or newsagent or can be ordered direct from the publisher. Just tick the titles you want and fill in the form below.

Prices and availability subject to change without notice.

HODDER AND STOUGHTON PAPERBACKS, PO Box 11, Falmouth, Cornwall.

Please send cheque or postal order for the value of the book, and add the following for postage and packing:

UK including BFPO – £1.00 for one book, plus 50p for the second book, and 30p for each additional book ordered up to a £3.00 maximum.

OVERSEAS INCLUDING EIRE – £2.00 for the first book, plus £1.00 for the second book, and 50p for each additional book ordered.
OR Please debit this amount from my Access/Visa Card (delete as appropriate).

Card Number | | | | | | | | | | | | | | | | |

AMOUNT £ ....

EXPIRY DATE ....

SIGNED ....

NAME ....

ADDRESS ....